Franciscus Columna
The Last Novella of Charles Nodier

Charles Nodier

Alpha Editions

This edition published in 2022

ISBN : 9789356156951

Design and Setting By
Alpha Editions
www.alphaedis.com
Email - info@alphaedis.com

As per information held with us this book is in Public Domain.
This book is a reproduction of an important historical work. Alpha Editions uses the best technology to reproduce historical work in the same manner it was first published to preserve its original nature. Any marks or number seen are left intentionally to preserve its true form.

Franciscus Columna

Charles Nodier (1780-1844)

Perhaps you remember our friend Abbot Lowrich whom we met in Ragusa, in Spalato, in Vienna, in Munich, in Pisa, in Bologna, and in Lausanne. He is an excellent fellow, who is most knowledgeable, but who knows a multitude of things that we would be happy to forget if we knew them like he does: the name of the printer of a bad book, the year of birth of a fool and a thousand other details of trivial importance. Abbot Lowrich has the glory of having discovered the real name of Kuicknackius, who was called Starkius, and not, please note, Polycarpus Starkius, who wrote eight fine hendecasyllables on the thesis of Kornmannus de ritibus (on rites) and on the thesis of Kornmannus de ritibus et doctrina scarabeorum (on rites and the doctrine of scarab beetles), but Martinus Starkius, the man who wrote thirty-two hendecasyllables on fleas. Apart from that, Abbot Lowrich deserves to be well known and liked; he is witty, has his heart in the right place, is actively and sincerely obliging, and he adds to these precious qualities a lively and singular imagination, which greatly embellishes his conversation, as long as it does not fall into enumerating minor biographical and bibliographical details. I am reconciled to this slight peccadillo of his, and whenever I meet Abbot Lowrich in my constant comings and goings across Europe, I run to him from afar. And I last met him no more than three months ago.

I had arrived at night at the Two Towers Hotel in Treviso, but I had only settled in very late, and I had not set foot in the town itself. In the morning, as I was going down the stairs, I saw in front of me one of those strange figures whose faces are visible from every angle. It was wearing a hat that defied all description, adjusted to its head in a way that was maladjusted, a red and green tie knotted like a scarf, a good four inches above the collar of the jacket on the left-hand side and a good four inches below it on the right, a pair of trousers brushed in a slipshod manner on one leg while the other leg billowed over the back of a boot with a sort of coquetry. It had with it a huge irremovable wallet in which lay so many titles of books, so many notices, so many plans, so many sketches, so many priceless treasures for a man of learning that, if he had dropped it, even a rag-and-bone man would not have picked it up. There were no two ways about it, it was Lowrich. "Lowrich!" I exclaimed, and we fell into each other's arms.

"I know where you're going," he said, after we had exchanged a few friendly words, and then, when I had learned that he too had only just arrived: "You asked for the address of a bookseller, and you were given that of Apostolo

Capoduro who resides in the strada dei Schiavoni. I'm going there too, but I don't hold out much hope, for I've visited his shop twice in ten years and never found books older than the novels of Abbot Chiari. That old bookshop has died the death, been ruined and sacked by barbarians. But did you have in mind something in particular to ask him for?"

"I'll admit to you," I answered, "that it would pain me to leave Northern Italy without taking with me 'The Dream of Poliphilus', of which I have heard it said that it is a most curious object and is to be found in Treviso if it is to be found anywhere."

"If it is to be found anywhere," he exclaimed, "is, to be sure, a prudent rider, for 'The Dream of Poliphilus', or, better still, Friar Francesco Colonna's 'Hypnerotomachia' is a book that old bibliographers call by the epithet: Albo corvo rarior. All I can say for sure is that if this white crow is to be found in any aviary, as we cannot but assume, it will definitely not be in Apostolo's. I think I'm sure enough of my facts to swear here by the household gods of Aldus Manutius the Elder (God keep him haloed in an everlasting glory) that, if this scamp Apostolo succeeds in providing you with a copy of the book in question in the 1499 first edition, for the second edition belongs, more or less, to the run-of-the-mill type of book, I hereby affirm that I'll make you a present of it out of my own purse, the contents of which this generous action on my part would cause to weigh considerably less."

Just then we entered the shop of Apostolo, who, his quill pen poised over a sheet of paper, seemed absorbed in deep meditation, though he at last grew aware of our presence, and appeared to joyfully recognize the unforgettable face of Abbot Lowrich. "Is it indeed the Lord, dear abbot," he said, hugging him, "who has sent you to extricate me from the most awkward predicament that I have ever found myself in? You cannot but know that I have been publishing, for some months now, the Adriatic Literary Gazette, which is, as all are agreed upon, the most erudite and witty of Europe's journals. Well! This rare scholarly journal, which is destined to have the world admire it and to get me back my fortune, is under threat of not appearing tomorrow for want of six small columns of serial, for which I have had recourse to my imagination tired out by study and business in vain. An evil spirit must have encompassed my ruin and sown disorder in my editor's office. The young muse who used to write my articles on moral education has gone into labour. The composer who was to let me have this morning a brand new type of cantata has written to say that it will take him at least a week to finish it, and the able financier who deals with questions of finance and political economy was sent to jail for non-payment of debt yesterday. For heaven's sake, my dear abbot, sit down at this table where I've sweated blood all night without my brain being able to yield a single line, and jot down five or six pages just as they come to you, if only a short story that won't have been used more than two or three times already."

"Wait one moment," Abbot Lowrich riposted. "We'll have time enough to deal with your affairs after we've dealt with our own. We did not come to you, my friend from Paris, and myself from the fjords of Norway, to make good a missing cantata by a lazy composer, or to dash off a pot boiler, but to see some of these books that are at least worth the trouble and expense of a journey, a good first edition duly documented, a well-preserved cinquecento rarity with its date of publication, a valuable volume printed by the Aldine Press in which its English and French bookbinders have deigned to arrange margins."

"As you please," replied Apostolo. "And I am all the more willing to consent to it as this inspection will not take us long. I have one work only worthy of being examined by connoisseurs like you. But what a work it is," he added, taking out of its triple wrapping an impressive looking folio. "What a work indeed," he went on, looking solemn, after he had quite detached it from its prison of wrapping paper. "A work to marvel at..." And he held out the book to Abbot Lowrich while giving him a look full of confidence and pride.

"Damnation!" murmured Lowrich, after having run his eye, as was his wont, over the unfamiliar treasure. Then he turned to me, but very different from what he had been the moment before, his arms hanging down at his side, his eye downcast, his forehead pale. "Damnation!" he muttered in French in a voice hardly raised and so that he could only be heard by me. "It's that damn book that I undertook to give you if it was here, the first edition of the Poliphilus... It's here, the traitor, and as fine as if it had just been printed. Things like this only happen to me..."

"Calm down," I answered, laughing. "Perhaps we'll get it for a price less than you think. And how much is Master Apostolo asking for this rarity?"

"Ah!" said Apostolo. "Times are hard and money is scarce. In times gone by I'd have asked fifty zecchini for it from Prince Eugene, sixty from the Duke of Abrantès, and a hundred from an Englishman. But today I have to give it away for four hundred wretched Milan pounds, or the exact equivalent of four hundred French francs. I can't even knock two quarantani off the price."

"May four hundred starving rats devour your books from first to last!" Lowrich interrupted furiously. "Who the devil has ever had four hundred francs asked of them for a bad book?"

"How dare you call this a bad book!" Apostolo spat back, almost as agitated as Lowrich. "It's a first edition of 1467, the first to appear in Treviso, and perhaps in Italy, a true masterpiece of typography and engraving, the illustrations in which can only be attributed to Raphael, an admirable work, the name of whose author has remained a mystery up until now, despite all erudite research, a one-off, or almost unique, that you yourself, abbot, perhaps did not know existed. And it pleases you to call that a bad book!"

Lowrich had calmed down during this vehement tirade. He had quietly sat down, placing his hat on the bookseller's table, and was wiping the sweat from his brow like a man exhausted by long and hard effort who has just found a good place to rest at his leisure.

"Have you finished, Apostolo?" he said in a calm tone of voice, in which, however, there could be detected a trace of I know not what malignant satisfaction. "The best thing I can hope for you is that you do no more to harm your kudos and your business interests from now on than you already have done. You have just said four very foolish things in as many words. If you had persisted, it would have taken me more than a day to recapitulate them one by one, and to do that would not leave me enough time to dictate that pot boiler, so, first of all: it isn't true that this book was printed in Treviso in 1467. It's an edition that was printed in Venice in 1499 from which the final page has been taken to deceive you as to the date of publication, and I didn't at first take note of that defect, which reduces the value of your copy by more than half, and therefore consider yourself fortunate in that I am able to remedy this fault, for blind chance allowed me to find the other day among some wrapping paper this precious end flyleaf, which I carefully kept in reserve for an opportunity to use it that I did not think would come so soon, so we'll presently see at what price I can let you have it."

So saying, Abbot Lowrich took from its cardboard cover the missing plagula, and carefully fitted it into the book. "This page fits my book perfectly," said Apostolo, "but I have to admit that it does change the nature of it somewhat. Where the devil did I get the idea that this was a Treviso first edition?"

"Never mind that," Lowrich continued, "we haven't finished yet. Let's get on to the second foolish thing you said: it isn't true that the drawings in this book can be attributed to Raphael, whether the edition dates back to 1467, or was only published in 1499, as has just been proved to you. Raphael was born in Urbino in 1483 and even the greatest admirers of this sublime painter cannot imagine him drawing so correctly and elegantly sixteen years before his birth. It must have been a different Raphael who drew these fine things, and as to him, my good Apostolo, there's only me who knows who he was. Wait. I've only counted up to two so far. Now we come to your third glaring error of fact: it isn't true that the author of this book has been till today a mystery to scholars. On the contrary, all scholars know, and the majority of non-scholars are not ignorant of the fact that it is the work of Francesco Colonna or Columna, a Dominican monk in the monastery of Treviso, where he died in 1467, whatever some scatterbrained writers of life stories have to say on the matter, who confuse him with Doctor Francesco di Colonia, whose name is almost homonymous with him and who survived him for all of sixty years. Both of them are buried only a few hundred paces from your shop, Apostolo. In view of what I've just said, I do not need to show you that you have made a fourth huge mistake, worse than the other three, by imagining that I did not know of the existence of your splendid tome, and I really don't know what's stopping me from proving to you that I know it by heart."

"Just this once," Apostolo replied smartly, "I dare you to recite it, for it is written in a language so heterogeneous that none of my friends from Treviso, Venice or Padua has dared to undertake to decipher a page of it, and if, as you say, you know it by heart, I'll give it you for nothing, a sacrifice besides I would be more than willing to make by reason of the excellent information that you have just given me, for I was on the point of announcing this volume in the Adriatic Literary Gazette in a misleading way and there was enough scope to make me lose forever the good and high flying reputation I enjoy as a bookseller."

"What you have just said yourself on the decidedly very strange style of our author," replied Abbot Lowrich, "and on the wasted efforts of so many scholars who have tried so hard to interpret it, is ample proof that what you are asking me for is a tiresome and fastidious demonstration that would take all day. And where would your pot boiler be if I were to recite the Hypnerotomachia from start to finish? I nevertheless will accept your challenge if you are willing to content yourself with trying an experiment which is no less conclusive, but would be quicker and easier. The chapter headings in your book are already too numerous and would try your patience, so I will only undertake to tell you their initial letters, beginning with the first, on which I see that you have just placed your finger."

"Let it be done as you say it should," said Apostolo. "And the first letter of the first chapter is…"

"A P," said Lowrich. "And now look for the second."

The list was long, but the abbot went down it to the final and thirty-eighth chapter without being disconcerted for a moment and without making a single mistake.

"Guessing an initial letter out of twenty-four to choose from, can be thought of as an outlandish freak of good fortune, with the devil well out of it," Apostolo observed sadly, "but to do that same trick thirty-eight times on the trot, the game must be rigged. Take this tome, abbot, and we'll never talk of it again."

"May God keep me, oh phoenix of bibliophiles," answered Lowrich, "from taking advantage to such an extent of your innocence and candour! What you have just witnessed is nothing more than a trick hardly worthy of a schoolboy, and which shortly you will be able to do just as well as I can. Know then that the author of this book judged it meet to conceal in the initial letters of his chapter headings his name, his profession and his secret love, so that, joined together, these letters make a sentence, the secret of which I cannot advise you to seek in the Universal Biography in Paris, as it would make you lose the wager that I have just won. Besides, that simple and touching sentence is easy to remember: Poliam frater Franciscus Columna peramavit, Friar Francesco Colonna loved Polia very much. Now you know as much about this as Bayle and Prosper Marchand."

"How strange it is," Apostolo said, half to himself. "This friar of the Dominicans fell in love. There's a story there somewhere."

"Why not?" replied Lowrich. "Pick up your quill again and let's look for your pot boiler, being as you have to have one."

Apostolo made himself comfortable on his chair, dipped his quill in the ink, and wrote what follows, starting with the title I have wandered away from in too long a digression:

FRANCISCUS COLUMNA, A BIBLIOGRAPHICAL NOVELLA.

The Colonna family is certainly one of the most important in Rome and in Italy, but not all its branches were equally prosperous. Sciarra Colonna, a passionate Ghibelline, who made Boniface VIII the prisoner of the Agnani, and got carried away, in the ecstasy of his victory, to the point of slapping the Supreme Pontiff, was made to suffer cruelly for his violence under John XXII. He was exiled from Rome for life in 1328, had his children stripped of their nobility as was he, and all his worldly goods confiscated to enrich Stefano Colonna, his brother, who had never abandoned the party of the Guelphs. The descendants of the unfortunate Sciarra died, as he himself did, in Venice, in obscurity and poverty. By 1444 only one of them was left alive to inherit such misery. Francesco Colonna, born at the start of that year was twice made an orphan, losing his father, killed on the day before he was born, and his mother who died giving birth to him. Francesco, piously adopted by none other than Jacopo Bellini, the famous history painter, and tenderly brought up with his own children, showed himself worthy of the generous care he had had from his adoptive father and from the illustrious brothers of the latter, Giovanni and Gentile Bellini. From the age of eighteen onwards, he repeated in the history of painting the precocious triumphs of the young Mantegna: Giotto had another rival. Fate, however, which did not cease to dog Francesco's life, did not allow his young successes to be wreathed in glory, and it is under the name of Mantegna or one of the Bellinis that the masterpieces of his brush are admired today.

Painting, however, was far from being the exclusive focus of his studies and affections. He only accorded it an importance that was secondary among the arts that beautify man's earthly sojourn. Architecture, on the other hand, which raises monuments to the gods, solemn intermediaries between earth and heaven, took up the greater part of his thoughts, but he did not look for its laws and marvels in the gigantic creations of contemporary art, the bizarre and often grotesque whims and fancies of a fantasy, lacking, according to him, the outward grace of reason and taste. Carried forward by the motion of the Renaissance, which was by then starting to make itself felt in Italy, Francesco only still belonged as far as faith went to this modern world renewed by Christianity. He wholly admired Antiquity and worshipped at its shrine, and a strange alliance had taken place in his mind between the beliefs of a religious man and the aesthetics of a pagan. He took this preoccupation too far to see in modern languages themselves nothing other than rustic jargons more or less totally corrupted by Barbarians, which were only good to allow men to negotiate the material necessities of life, and which were not capable of rising to translate eloquently or poetically ideas and feelings. The result of this was that he had forged for his own usage a sort of intimate dialect in which Italian only served to define certain elements of syntax and the odd soft inflexion, but which was much more redolent of the followers of Homer or of Titus Livius and Lucan than of Petrarch and Boccaccio. This singular turn of mind, which was at that time the defining hallmark of original powers of organisation and a personality destined, to all appearances, to exert a great influence on the century, had isolated Francesco from the rest of the world. He gave to it the general impression of being a melancholic seer who had fallen prey to an illusory genius that had rendered him insensitive to the gentle ways of life in society. He was sometimes seen nevertheless in the palazzo of the illustrious Leonora Pisani, the heiress, at the age of eight and twenty, to the greatest fortune ever known in the whole of the Veneto after that of her cousin Polia, the only daughter of the last of the Poli in Treviso. The house of Leonora was then the sanctuary of poetry and the arts, and this muse's influence caused irresistibly to congregate around her all the talents of her age. It was soon noticed that Francesco was going there more often, although more absorbed in his daydreams and sadder than usual, but his visits suddenly became less frequent, and then he stopped coming altogether.

Polia dei Poli, whom I have just mentioned, was then in the palazzo of the Pisani family, where Leonora had decided her to come to spend the mad weeks of the Carnival. Eight years younger than her cousin, and more beautiful than Leonora was herself, Polia, dedicated, as were a great number of young ladies of noble birth, to serious studies, profited from her sojourn in the capital of the scholarly world to improve herself in areas of knowledge today quite alien to her sex, and the habit of these solemn meditations had imparted to her face something cold and austere which passed for pride. It was not really to be wondered at, however, for Polia was the last surviving remnant of the ancient Lelia family in Rome, from whom she was descended by way of Lelius Maurus, the founder of Treviso. She was brought up under the watchful eye of an imperious and haughty father, so proud of the splendour of his race, that he would have considered the marriage of his daughter to the greatest prince in Italy as marrying below her station, and besides, it was known that the treasures that she would inherit one day could suffice for the dowry of a queen. She had nonetheless granted to Francesco, in their first meetings, a few signs of almost affectionate benevolence, but, as time went on, she seemed to have gradually prescribed for herself a reserve that was severe, not to say disdainful, and when he stopped showing himself at the palazzo Pisani, she no longer bothered with him.

It was during the course of the month of February 1466. Spring, often early in that fair region, was beginning to fill it with all its favours. Polia was about to return to Treviso, and her cousin multiplied around her the various festivities that might enhance her sojourn in Venice and make it harder for her to leave. One day had been taken up by gondola outings on the Grand Canal and on that broad and deep arm of it that separates the Serenissima from the solitude of its Lido. But Francesco had not been overlooked in Leonora Pisani's invitations, and the letter which he had had from her contained such amiable and touching reproaches as to his long absence that for him to refuse would have been inconceivable. Polia was besides, as we have pointed out, on the point of leaving for Treviso, and we may safely assume that Francesco wanted to see her again in spite of the habitual coldness of her welcome. Thinking more and more about the drastic change that had so soon come about in the relations between them, he had ended up by persuading himself that this capricious metamorphosis was due to something other than hate. He found himself then on the steps of the palazzo Pisani, the general assembly point for the departure of the gondolas. The ladies, wearing masks and identical dominos, came out in a crowd from the hallway at the agreed upon signal, and each of them went to choose, as custom decreed, with the familiar decency imparted by disguise, the companion that they were pleased to attach to themselves for the journey. This way of doing things, more gracious and better understood than the one that has taken its place in balls and assemblies, also had less serious disadvantages, women never being more attentive to the preservation of their reputations than on those too rare occasions when they are wholly responsible for maintaining them. So Francesco was waiting, motionless and with downcast eyes, for someone to take notice of him, when a pretty gloved hand came to rest on his arm. He welcomed the unknown woman with modest and respectful assiduity, and led her to the gondola already prepared to receive them. A moment later the elegant flotilla was moving to the rhythmical splash of the oars on the calm and polished face of the canal.

The lady, who was seated at Francesco's left, remained silent for a time, as if she had needed to recollect herself and to master, before she spoke, some involuntary emotion. Then she undid the ties of her mask, threw it back upon her shoulder, and gazed at Francesco with that gentle and serious assurance that self-consciousness gives to elevated souls. It was Polia. Francesco trembled and felt a sudden shiver pass through all his veins, for he had expected nothing like this. Then he leaned his head and covered his eyes with his hand in the fear that it might be a kind of defilement for her to look at Polia so closely.

"This mask is useless," said Polia. "There is no reason for me to take advantage of the custom which allows me to keep it. Our friendship does not need it and its feelings are too pure for it to blush to express them. Do not be surprised, Francesco," she continued after a moment of silence, "to hear me speak of my friendship for you after so many days of rigorous constraint in which I may have given you grounds to doubt it. My sex is subject to certain laws of decorum which do not permit it to manifest its most legitimate sympathies to the interpretations of the crowd, and there is nothing more difficult than to feign to a correct extent an indifference one does not feel. Today I shall leave Venice, and although I am destined to live very near to you, it is quite probable that we will never see each other again. Henceforth there is no longer any possible way for us to communicate with each other than by memory, and I did not want to leave you with a false idea of me, or to take away of you an anxious and painful idea that would trouble my peace of mind. I have provided for the first eventuality by giving you an explanation that I thought I owed you. I expect from your sincerity that you will reassure me as to the second point by confiding in me, which is something that you owe to me perhaps. Don't be alarmed, Francesco. You yourself shall be the sole judge of whether my questions are appropriate or not."

Just before she had said this Francesco had opened his downcast eyes. He dared to look at Polia. He drank in her words avidly. "Ah!" he cried. "As God is my witness, my soul has no secret that does not belong to you."

"Your soul has a secret," replied Polia, "a secret that besets your friends and that certain people among those you love best may find it of use to fathom. Endowed with all the advantages that augur for a happy future: youth, ingenio, knowledge and already glory, you nonetheless abandon yourself to the languor of a mysterious sadness, you are consumed by a secret care, you neglect the works on which your reputation is based, you flee from a world that seeks you out in order to hide in almost opaque solitude days that so much success should make resplendent and, finally, if the rumours that are circulating are worthy of credence, you are on the point of breaking entirely with human society and retiring to a monastery. Is what I have just said to you true?"

Francesco seemed agitated by a thousand conflicting emotions. He needed a few moments to gather his strength. "Yes," he replied, "that is true. At least, all of it was true this morning. An event which has happened since has changed the course of my ideas without changing my resolutions. I will go to a monastery and my commitment is irrevocable, but I will go with a mind that is fully consoled and joyful, for my existence is complete and I cannot conceive of any other one so happy on earth that it would render me jealous. Born into obscurity and poverty, but stronger than my fate, I had only measured my unhappiness by the immensity of the void into which my heart had plunged. This void has been filled by the most delightful of hopes: you will remember me!"

Polia looked at him sweetly. "I want," she said, "not to see in your words a simple game of the imagination or one of those flattering condescensions of courtesy with which people think to have repaid friendship. It seems to me that this artificial language of the cold should not be applied to us. I therefore think that I begin to grasp a fraction of the things that you have said to me, with the exception of your resolve, but," she added smiling, "I do not understand them sufficiently."

"You shall understand them better," said Francesco, encouraged, "for I shall tell you everything. Forgive however the troubled nature and the lack of resolution in my words, for, of all the vicissitudes in my life, this is the most unexpected. The strange position into which I was born, without parents, without a guardian, almost without a friend, fallen from a great name and an independent fortune, would doubtless be enough to explain my natural melancholy. It's a cruel thing to say to yourself that your unhappiness started in the cradle and stayed with you the rest of your life. But that idea was the first I was able to be aware of. I had to acquit myself of the material debt of gratitude before I could think for a single moment of myself, and I do not need to tell you that I succeeded in that. From that time on my courage grew. I had few regrets for the grandeur and the opulence that had faded away forever. I went further. I congratulated myself sometimes, in my childish pride, on owing all my illustriousness to myself, and on being able one day to force the family that had rejected me to envy the celebrity of my once repudiated name. Such are the illusions of inexperience and vanity. One day was to destroy all and to recall me to misfortune and oblivion. Alas!" Francesco went on, "this is the mystery your overly benevolent curiosity has expressed the desire to know, and which reason made for me a law of keeping hidden in my breast. But how can I dare to reveal to you those sad and deep secrets of sick hearts that wisdom and philosophy regard as a puerile infirmity of the mind, and over which the elevation of your character keeps you too high for you to deign to bestow on them any other feeling apart from pity? I fell in love…"

Hereupon Francesco stopped for a time, but reassured by a look from Polia, he continued as follows:

"I loved without having thought about it, without appreciating the consequences of my extravagant passion, without fearing them for the future, for I lived completely in the impressions of the present. I loved a woman who would be universally recognizable were I to depict the rare qualities that she is clothed with, combining with beauty all the perfections of intelligence and soul, and that heaven seems only to have entrusted to earth to remind us of the ineffable joy of the condition we have lost. I loved her without remembering that she was, of all aristocrats, the noblest, of all the affluent, the most affluent and that I was only Francesco Colonna, the unknown pupil of Bellini, and that all my efforts to be happy in my work would only ever lead me to the acquisition of a sterile reputation. Such is the effect of that passion that dazzles, that blinds, that kills. When reflection had restored me to myself, when I had sounded with a frightened eye, with the bitter laughter of despair, the chasm towards which I had made so much headway without even knowing it, it was too late to go back: I was lost. The first thought of a wretch is to die. That thought is as commodious as it is natural because it answers all questions and remedies all inconveniences. But might not this desperate death, far from hastening to bring about the day when I may draw nearer to her in a better world, separate me from her forever? It was a totally new idea that held back my arm when it was ready to strike; I took in the future that my inability to endure a few days without her was going to deprive me of. I was painfully condemned to live without hope, but without fear, to reach that moment when two souls, freed from all the ties that have weighed down on them, look for each other, recognize each other and are then brought together for all time. I made of her I loved an object of worship my whole life long. I raised to her an inviolable altar in my heart and dedicated myself to her as an everlasting sacrifice. Can I say that, under my invincible sadness, this plan, once decided upon, was mingled with some joy? I grasped that this marriage, which started with widowhood to end up having, was perhaps preferable to ordinary marriages, which shatter on bad days. I no longer saw in the years that remained to me to spend among men anything other than a long engagement that death would crown with an eternal felicity. I felt the need to isolate myself from the world to recollect myself in a nevertheless delightful feeling of austerity that I would not have to share, and that is why I embraced the duties of the would-be monk. May God pardon his creature's weakness! The oath that will bind me to Him in three days' time is the oath that will bind me indissolubly to her I love and that will only give me rights over her in heaven. Allow me to repeat, by way of conclusion, that the accomplishment of this plan will now cost nothing to my resignation since a generous compassion has let me conceive of the hope of not being forgotten."

"In only three days!" exclaimed Polia. "In effect," she went on, "I have had too little time to reflect on the secret you have just confided in me to dare to form an opinion and even less a judgement, but it seems to me that if the woman for whom you resolved to do such things does not remain in ignorance of them as I was ignorant of them before now, she did not deserve to inspire them."

"She is ignorant of them," replied Francesco, "because she does not know that I love her. Oh! Without a doubt, my heart could have found ineffable consolations in the idea that my love was known to her, that she was not entirely insensitive to it, and that she might, at the very least, remember it with pity! Of all the torments of love, the most cruel perhaps is to remain an unknown quantity to the person one loves; of all the feelings one inspires that dull feeling of indifference for a stranger is perhaps the most painful that love has to fear. But why throw into a heart that is peaceful and happy pains that one is hardly capable of bearing oneself? Either my passion will be rejected, as I suppose, and what will I have gained from having this sad intuition confirmed, or it will be mutual and I will have to suffer for both of us. What am I saying: suffer for both of us? My despair is my life since I have found in myself enough strength to live with it. Hers would have killed me already."

"You take your suppositions too far, Francesco," Polia replied buoyantly. "Who can know if she does not feel the same sorrows and the same anguish as you do? Who can know if she does not aspire to find a moment to tell you that? What would you say if this noble and rich female whose shine dazzles you, but whose soul is probably no calmer than yours, what would you say, Francesco, if she came to offer you her hand freely, if, subject to a sway both respectable and inflexible, she came to promise it you in marriage?"

"What would I say, Polia?" Francesco answered with cold dignity, "I would refuse it. In order to dare love her I love, one needs to be to a certain extent worthy of her, and my most constant application has been to ennoble my soul so that it would be closer to hers. What right would I have to accept the perks of a high position that society denies me? With what impudence could I take my seat at the banquet of fortune, I who have only obscurity and misery as my prerogatives? Oh! I would a thousand times rather have the horrid sorrow that consumes me than the shameful reputation of an adventurer rebuffed by the world and made rich by love!"

"I had not finished," Polia broke in. "You are overscrupulous, but I understand your scruple and share it. The world as it goes demands odd sacrifices and one would perhaps be asked of you by reason of your character, but a character of the same calibre as yours might answer with a different sort of denial. Greatness and fortune are accidents of fate one can get rid of if one wants to. The artist and the poet are everywhere the same. Everywhere they have success and glory, but beyond an arm of the sea the woman who is rich and titled who has known how to shake off these vain privileges of birth is no more than a woman. If this woman came to say to you: I renounce my greatness, I abandon my fortune, I am ready to become even humbler and poorer than you, and to commit to your charge, as to my sole source of support, the whole of my life's destiny, what would you say to that, Francesco?"

"I would fall at her knees," said Francesco, "and answer thus: Heavenly angel, keep the rank and the advantages that heaven has conferred on you; you must be and stay what you are, and the wretch who would be capable of letting himself be carried along by this tender and sublime urge of your heart would never have deserved to occupy a place in it. He can no longer raise himself up to you except by constant resignation, easy for one who hopes, and especially for one who is loved. It is not I who would make you come down from the position in which God did not put you without a motive, in order to submit you to the varying fortunes of an anxious existence, poisoned by needs incessantly renewed, and perhaps one day by incurable regrets. My happiness is complete now. It exceeds all my hopes since you have granted to me all that you could take from the duties that your name imposes on you. You love me, I'd add, and you will always love me since you have not recoiled from resolving to give your life to mine. Your life, my beloved, I accept and take as a sacred pledge for which I will render an account before my Lord and Judge, for life is short, even for those who suffer, whatever weak hearts have to say about it. This earth is just a place of transit where souls come to be tested, and if your soul, as faithful as it is devoted, stays married to mine during the years that time still allows us, the whole of eternity is ours…"

Polia was silent for a time. "Yes! Yes!" she exclaimed exaltedly. "God has not instituted a holier or more inviolable sacrament. It is in this way that a love such as yours must have reconciled its hopes and its duties in a marriage of the heart that the rest of mankind does not know, and your heavenly spouse would speak to you as I speak to you if she had heard you."

"She has heard me, Polia," Francesco replied, letting his head at that moment fall into his hands with a torrent of tears.

"So," Polia went on, as if she had not understood the last words he had spoken, "you will assume in three days the habit of one of the religious orders to be found in Venice?"

"In Treviso," said Francesco. "I have not gone as far as to forbid myself the happiness of still seeing her sometimes."

"In Treviso, Francesco? There you only know me…"

"Only you!" said Francesco.

At that moment the hand of the young princess found itself joined to that of the young painter and the princess spoke. "We did not notice," she said smiling, "that the gondola was stopping and that it has already returned to the palazzo of the Pisani. Now we have nothing further to say to each other on earth. Our final farewell, however, is not without sweetness if we have understood each other correctly, and our first heavenly meeting will be even sweeter."

"Goodbye forever!" said Francesco.

"Goodbye for always!" said Polia. Then she re-attached her mask and got down from the gondola.

The following day Polia was in Treviso. Three days later they tolled at the monastery of the Dominicans that symbolic funeral knell which announces the profession of faith of a new postulant and his death to the world. Polia spent the day in her oratory.

Francesco acquiesced easily to his new destiny. Sometimes he looked back on his talk with Polia as a dream, but, more often, he went over the finest details of it with a childlike enthusiasm, and he went as far as to pat himself on the back for having given rise to, in his misery, a love that was oblivious to the ups and downs of fortune and of age. He accustomed himself after only a few days to divide his time between the duties of a religious and the leisured labour of an artist, at times painting those pure and naive frescos which may still be admired in the monastery of the Dominicans, though the cavalier arrogance of modern art has let them deteriorate, at times writing down in a book, the favourite object of his studies, all the impressions susceptible to him because of his talent and above all of his love. He had taken as the frame for this vast and bizarre work, in which he hoped to live again in his entirety, the somewhat vague form of a dream, and there could be nothing more apt, according to him, to represent, in its apparent disorder, the haphazard ideas of a solitary. We know that, due to one of the rare moments in which he was allowed to have a tender exchange of words with Polia, she had assured him that she would accept his dedication to her of this strange poem, and he tells us himself that she helped him with advice. So it was that he gave up completely the use of the vernacular Italian in which he had first thought out his plan and started it, and 'lasciando il princiniato stilo', he gave himself over to that scholarly language where there were neither models nor imitators for him and the words of which were furnished to his flowing quill by his erudite interest in ancient matters. A year went by in these sweet works mixed with sweet illusions, and Francesco had just put the finishing touches to his work, when the most distressing and heartbreaking news came through the walls where the Dominicans were. The young Antonio Grimani, later admiral and doge of Venice, but already the most brilliant of its nobles and its highest hope, had just asked for the hand of Polia in marriage, and, it was added, the hand of Polia had been granted to him.

It was the day that Francesco was to present his book to Polia. He stood up to the blow that had just struck him, went to her palazzo and stopped on the threshold of her apartment. "Come, my brother," said Polia when she saw him. "Come to communicate to us these secret wonders of your art, a true treasure that Christian humility refuses to the world, and which is to be confided only to us." At the same time she shooed away her women and her servants, and Francesco was alone with her.

His legs gave way under him, a cold sweat broke out on his brow, his arteries beat violently, his breast swelled fit to burst.

Polia raised her eyes from the manuscript to look at the monk. Francesco's pallor, the bloody halo girding his eyes worn out with crying, the shaking of his livid hands hanging loosely, revealed to her what was happening in the heart of her lover. She smiled proudly.

"You have heard," she said, "of my forthcoming marriage with prince Antonio Grimani?"

"Yes, madam," replied Francesco.

"And what did you think, Francesco, of this alliance?"

"That no man is worthy to contract such an alliance with you, but that the prince Antonio had more rights than anyone, and that the marriage appeared to be what Venice wanted... and what you yourself wanted. May it always bring you happiness!"

"I refused it this morning," said Polia.

Francesco looked at her as if to seek in Polia's eyes if her mouth had not betrayed her thought.

"You know better than anyone," Polia went on, "that I have pledged my troth elsewhere and that my decision to do so is irrevocable. But I must forgive your suspicions for yours is guaranteed by the oath that binds you to an altar and I have never given you a guarantee like that. Listen, Francesco. Tomorrow is the anniversary of the day you made your first vows, and it will be during the last morning mass that you will render them even more binding and more sacred by renewing them before the Lord. Have you, now a year has passed, changed your way of thinking about the nature of this sacrifice and the need for it?"

"No, no, Polia!" cried Francesco, falling to his knees.

"It is enough," continued Polia. "My thinking has not changed either. I shall be present tomorrow at the last morning mass, and I shall support with all the strength of my soul the vow that you will repeat then, so that henceforth you will know, Francesco, that between the heart of Polia and inconstancy there are also perjury and sacrilege."

Francesco tried to reply, but when the words came to his lips, Polia had disappeared.

The young monk found it almost as difficult to bear his joy as he did his misfortune. He felt that he no longer had enough strength to be happy, for the mainspring of his life, worn by so many conflicting emotions, had almost reached breaking point.

The following morning, at the final mass, when the monks entered the choir, Polia was sitting in her usual place, in the first row of benches set aside for the nobility. She got up and went to kneel in the middle of the pavement of the central nave.

Francesco had noticed her. He renewed his vows with an assured voice, went back down the altar steps, and prostrated himself on the floor. At the moment of the elevation of the host, he stretched out completely, throwing his crossed hands before his head.

Once mass was over, Polia left the church. The monks passed, one after the other, before the sanctuary, genuflecting deeply. But Francesco did not leave his position, and no-one was taken aback, for he had often been seen to prolong like this, in a motionless ecstasy, the duration of his prayer.

When the evening service came, Francesco had not changed his posture. A young friar came out of the choir stalls, approached him, bent down to him and took one of his hands in his, pulling his body towards him to recall it to its accustomed duties. Then he got up again, and, turning towards the assembled monks, said: "He's dead!"

This event, one of those which are so swiftly effaced in the collective memory of a new generation, had happened more than thirty-one years before when, on a winter evening in 1498, a gondola stopped in front of the shop of Aldo Pio Manucci, whom we refer to as the Elder. A moment later a visit from the princess Hippolita Polia of Treviso was announced in the study of the scholarly printer. Aldo ran to meet her, ushered her in, made her sit down, and was struck by admiration and respect for this celebrated beauty, whom half a century of life and sorrows had rendered more solemn, without taking anything away from her brilliance.

"Wise Aldo," she said to him after having had placed on his table a bag containing 2,000 gold coins and a weighty manuscript, "you will be in the eyes of the most remote posterity, the most erudite and skilful printer of all time and the author of this book that I am entrusting you with will leave behind the renown of the greatest painter and the greatest poet of this century now drawing to a close. You are the sole repository of this treasure, which I will ask you to give me back once your art has reproduced it. I have not wanted to deprive of its presence completely those minds favoured by heaven who know how to view the concepts of genius, but I have waited, to multiply the copies of it, the moment I could turn to a great printer. You know now, wise Aldo, what I expect of you: a masterpiece worthy of your name and capable just by itself of perpetuating your memory through ages to come. When this gold has been used up, I will bring more." Afterwards Polia got up and leaned with both hands on the women who had come with her. Aldo followed her to her gondola, showing his agreement with her by respectful gestures, but without talking to her, because he was not ignorant of the fact that, having lived in total solitude for more than thirty years, she had eschewed both the business and the conversation of men.

The book we must consider here is entitled the 'Hypnerotomachia di Poliphilo, sive pugna d'amore in sogno', that is to say 'Love's combat in a dream' and not 'The Combat of Love and Sleep' as Mister Ginguené, author of 'The Literary History of Italy', has in error translated it. We do not pretend, heaven forbid, that Mr Ginguené, author of 'The Literary History of Italy', did not know Italian. We are more indulgent towards talent's lapses.

"Sign that as you will," said Lowrich getting up. "I am not in the habit of putting my name to such trifles, and, as God is my witness, I have never granted such lightweight stories to sellers of books for any other purpose than to get books."

"May all the stories that you have before you," said Apostolo, "go to enrich your library with a volume like this one! It is yours and I owe it to you twice over."

"It is mine," said Lowrich, taking hold of it enthusiastically. "Or rather it belongs to you," he went on gaily, passing it from his hands to mine. "I promised it to you this morning!"

And so it is that the most magnificent copy of the Poliphilus, the giant of my Lilliputian collection, figures in it today nec pluribus impar. I submit it voluntarily to the gazes of book lovers, who cannot stop themselves from seeing in it a magnificent book… and one I did not pay the earth for!

Milton Keynes UK
Ingram Content Group UK Ltd.
UKHW042114220324
439862UK00004B/420